THE STUPIDS STEP OUT

Story by
HARRY ALLARD
Pictures by
JAMES MARSHALL

HOUGHTON MIFFLIN COMPANY BOSTON

Library of Congress Cataloging in Publication Data

Allard, Harry
  The Stupids step out.

  SUMMARY: The Stupid family and their dog Kitty
have a fun-filled day doing ridiculous things.
  (1. Humorous stories) I. Marshall, James,
1942– Illus. II. Title.
PZ7.A413St   (E)   73-21698
ISBN 0-395-18513-0 (rnf.)
ISBN 0-395-25377-2 (pbk.)

Printed in the United States of America
WOZ   30 29

For Bill and Silvia Crockett

One day Stanley Q. Stupid had an idea.

This was unusual.

"Calling all Stupids!" Stanley shouted.

Mrs. Stupid, Buster Stupid, Petunia Stupid, and the Stupids' wonderful dog Kitty all crawled out from under the rug.

"The Stupids are stepping out today," said Stanley.

The Stupids were delighted.

"Let's go upstairs and get ready," said Mrs. Stupid.

The two Stupid children climbed onto the banister.

"Up we go!" squealed Petunia.

They did not move. They wondered why.

"Bath time!" said Mrs. Stupid.

"Everyone into the tub," ordered Mr. Stupid.

"But where's the water?" asked Petunia.

"Don't be stupid," said Stanley. "If we fill
up the tub, our clothes will get wet."

"Listen to your father," said Mrs. Stupid.

"Mother," said Buster. "Your new hat is meowing."
"Of course it is, Buster," said Mrs. Stupid. "I'm wearing the cat."

"First let's stop at Grandfather and Grandmother Stupid's house," said Stanley. "They'll be so happy to see us."

UNCLE BORIS

"Don't forget the stockings I knitted for you,"

said Mrs. Stupid to her husband.

"I have them on, dear," said Mr. Stupid.

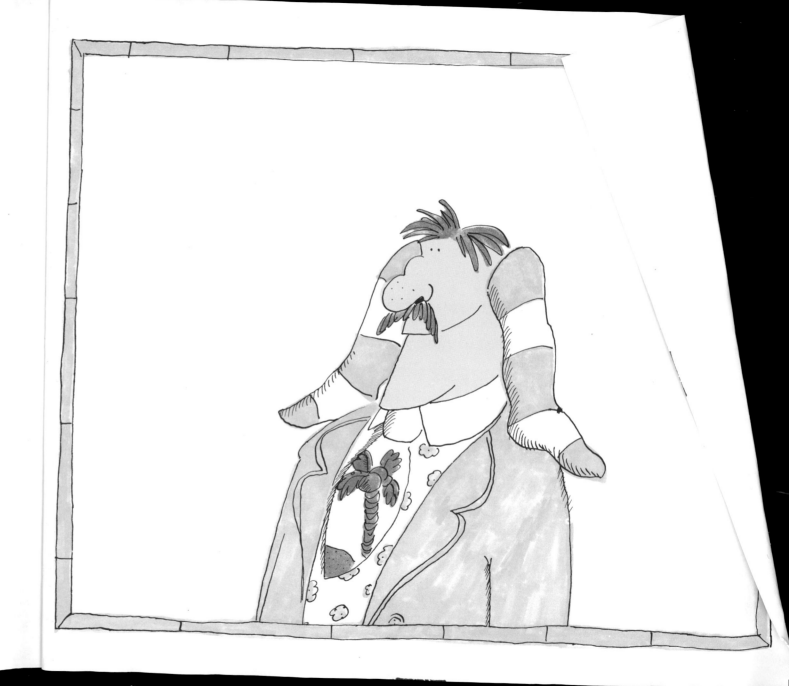

UNCLE BORIS

"Don't forget the stockings I knitted for you,"
said Mrs. Stupid to her husband.
"I have them on, dear," said Mr. Stupid.

"First let's stop at Grandfather and Grandmother Stupid's house," said Stanley. "They'll be so happy to see us."

"Who are you?" asked Grandfather at the door.

"I'm your son Stanley," said Mr. Stupid,

"and this is my wonderful family."

"Where's Grandmother Stupid?" asked Petunia.

"Where she always is," said her grandfather.

"She's in the closet."

"Hello children," Grandmother sang out through the keyhole. "How nice of you to come and see me."

It was a lovely visit.

"We must be off now," said Stanley.

"Come again," said Grandfather Stupid at the door, "whoever you are."

While Kitty was parking the car, Stanley Stupid

saw something amusing.

"Look at those funny-looking people in the window,"

he said to his family.

"Yes, they are certainly stupid looking,"

said Mrs. Stupid.

"Don't stare at them, children. It's impolite."

"I'm hungry," Petunia whined.

"So am I," said her father. "How about a delicious mashed potato sundae?"

"Um, um," exclaimed Buster, smacking his lips. "Mashed potatoes and butterscotch syrup."

When the Stupids had gobbled up the last of their mashed potato sundaes, they went home.

"Time to get ready for bed," said Mrs. Stupid.

The Stupids put on their sleeping clothes.

"Don't we look handsome," said Mr. Stupid.

When the Stupids were all tucked into bed, Mrs. Stupid gave her husband a kiss on the cheek. "Thank you for the lovely day, dear," she said. "It certainly has been fun."